For Mum, Dad and Meg
~ M B

LITTLE TIGER PRESS

An imprint of Magi Publications

1 The Coda Centre, 189 Munster Road, London SW6 6AW

www.littletigerpress.com

First published in Great Britain 2005

Text and illustrations copyright © Matt Buckingham 2005

Matt Buckingham has asserted his right to be identified
as the author and illustrator of this work under
the Copyright, Designs and Patents Act, 1988

A CIP catalogue record for this book
is available from the British Library

All rights reserved • ISBN 1 84506 198 5

Printed in Singapore by Tien Wah Press Pte.

10 9 8 7 6 5 4 3 2 1

The Not So Abominable Snowman

Matt Buckingham

LITTLE TIGER PRESS
London

Have you ever heard of the Abominable Snowman?
There are lots of them, you know. They live high
in the mountains, in the deep, white snow.

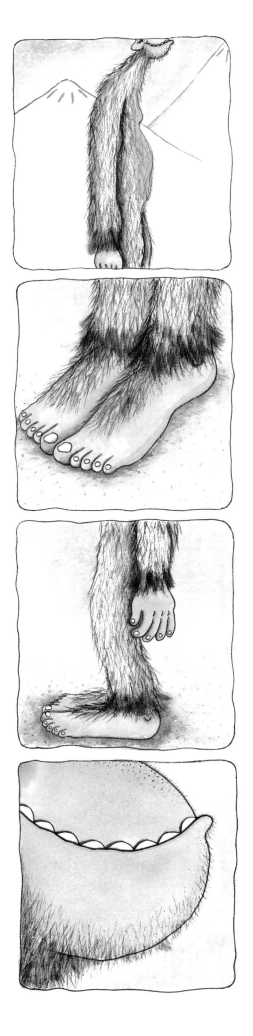

They're covered in hair

and have huge feet,

long strong arms

and gnashing white teeth.

Bert was an abominable snowman. He liked
the snowy mountains, but he also liked to play
in the thick forests far below. There he'd run,
jump, climb, crawl and chase butterflies.

One day Bert was chasing two butterflies when
they landed on a rock. Quietly he crept towards them.
But on the other side of the rock was a little BOY.
What a fright! He'd never seen such a sight!

Bert quickly dived into a bush to hide.
"AAAAWWWWWW!" Spiky thorns covered
him from head to toe!

The little boy walked over to Bert. "I'm sorry,"
he said. "I didn't mean to scare you. My name's Tom.
Who are you?"

"I'm Bert, an abominable snowman," said Bert.

"Oh! You don't look abominable to me," said Tom.

While Tom pulled the thorns from Bert's foot he told Bert that he was worried about his father. "I'm waiting for him here while he climbs up the mountain, but he's been so long, something must be wrong."

"Let's look for him," said Bert and he lifted Tom on to his shoulders.

Dashing through the thick bamboo they
met a giant panda.

"Hello, panda," said Bert. "Have you
seen a grown man pass by?"

"He passed nearby, before climbing up high," the panda said, and he began to chew on some bamboo.

As Bert and Tom climbed higher, the thick forest turned
to grassy slopes. There they met a herd of cattle grazing.
    "Hello, yaks," said Bert. "Have you seen a grown
man pass by?"

"He walked this way, but didn't stay," said one
yak, and went back to munching the grass.

As the mountain grew steeper the snow became deeper. They saw a leopard slinking along.

"Hello, leopard," said Bert. "Have you seen a grown man pass by?"

The leopard stopped and pointed higher up.
"I was roaming about when I heard a shout,"
she said, before going on her way.

They were nearly at the top of the mountain but there was still no sign of Tom's father. Tom was very worried.

"We could do with some help," said Bert and he began to dance. THUMP! THUMP! THUMP! went his feet on the icy snow.

Suddenly they heard a faint rumble that grew into a deafening stampede. The ground began to shake as lots and lots of abominable snowmen appeared.

As soon as Bert had told his friends about Tom's father, the tallest snowmen clambered on to each other's shoulders to make a tower.

Bert climbed to the top. From
there he could see for miles.
Far, far away he spotted
some tracks in the snow.

"I know where he is. Follow me!"
said Bert, and he jumped to the ground,
picked Tom up and raced off.

They ran many many miles. When they finally
stopped, Bert dived into a hole in the snow.
The next snowman leapt after him, grabbing
Bert's feet. One by one all the snowmen followed.

The very last snowman dug his enormous
feet into the ground and held on tight.

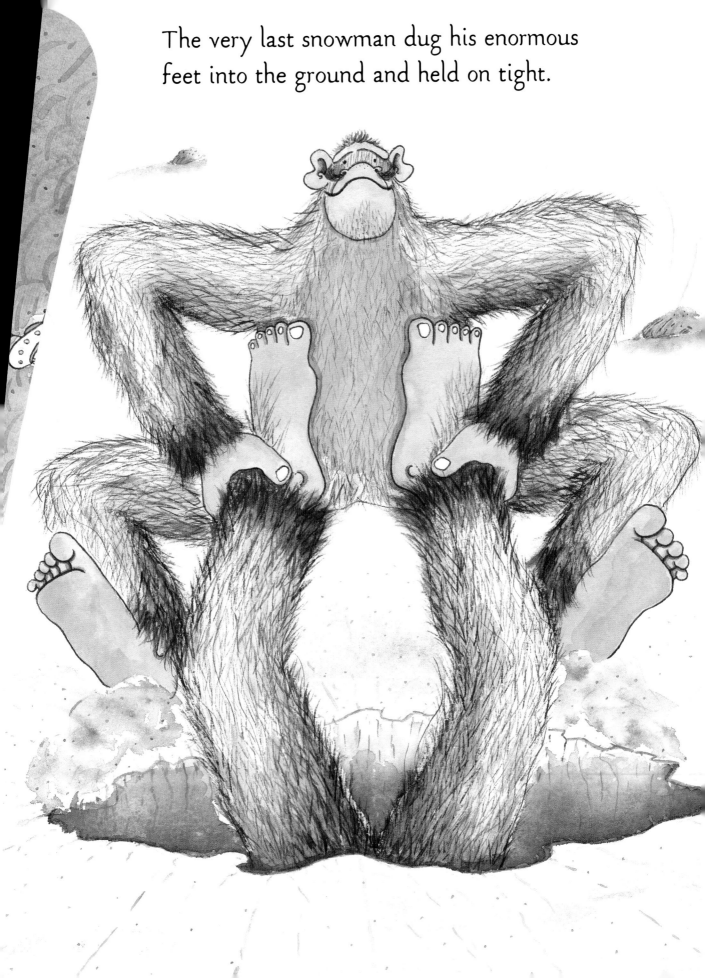

of the
crevasse,

in a cold heap,

was Tom's father.

"Hello," said Bert.
"I'm Bert. I've come
to help."

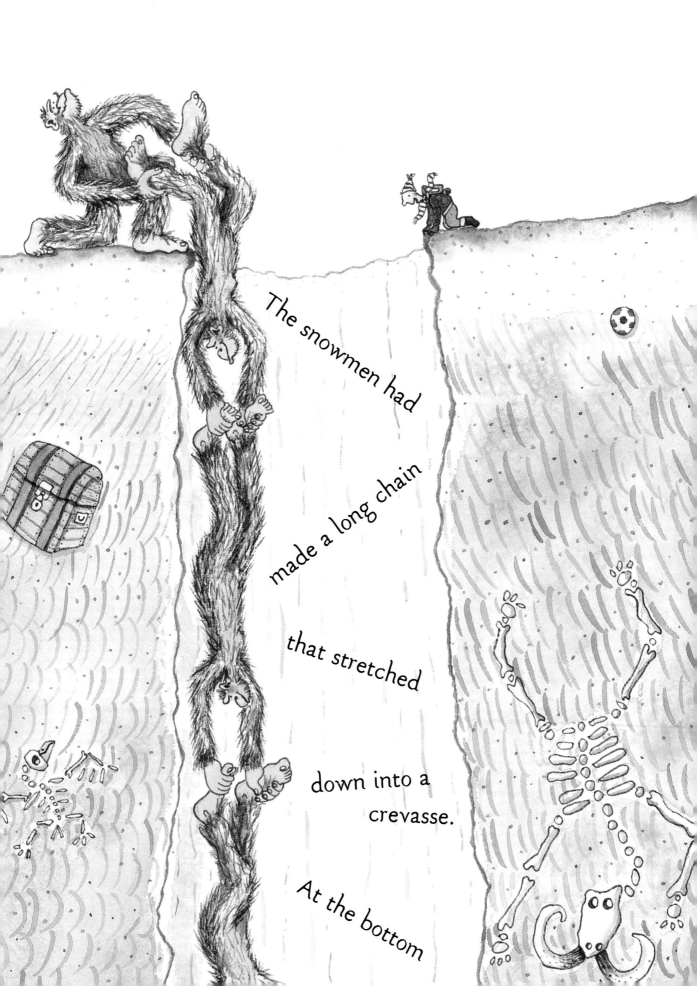

The snowmen had

made a long chain

that stretched

down into a
crevasse.

At the bottom

Bert carefully picked
up Tom's father and
gave a shout. The
last snowman hauled
everyone back to safety.

Tom was very pleased to see his father again.
He ran to him and gave him a big hug.
    "Oh Dad, I was so worried about you," he said.
Then he thanked Bert and the other snowmen.

Bert sadly waved goodbye to his new friends.
As Tom and his father made their way down
the mountain, he saw Tom point to some
huge footprints in the snow.

"You know, Dad?" Tom said. "Bert's not so
abominable, is he? In fact, none of them are."